My First Kitten

She listened again. The noise seemed to be coming from a cardboard box. She moved closer. Yes, the mewing was definitely coming from inside. She brushed off some potato peelings and lifted the lid. When she saw what was inside she gasped.

KITTENS!

If you enjoy **My First Kitten**, then you might want to read
My First Puppy

and
My First Pony

all by *Tessa Krailing.*

You could also try Tessa Krailing's **Petsitters Club,**
for even *more* animal adventure!

1. **Jilly the Kid**
2. **The Cat Burglar**
3. **Donkey Rescue**
4. **Snake Alarm!**
5. **Scruncher Goes Walkabout**
6. **Trixie and the Cyber Pet**
7. **Oscar the Fancy Rat**

TESSA KRAILING

My First Kitten

Inside illustrations by Neil Reed

Scholastic Children's Books,
Commonwealth House, 1-19 New Oxford Street,
London WC1A 1NU, UK
a division of Scholastic Ltd
London ~ New York ~ Toronto ~ Sydney ~ Auckland

Published in the UK by Scholastic Ltd, 1998

Text copyright © Tessa Krailing, 1998
Illustrations copyright © Neil Reed, 1998

ISBN 0 590 11127 2

Printed and bound by Mackays of Chatham plc, Chatham, Kent

2 4 6 8 10 9 7 5 3 1

Chapter 1

A Bit of Old Rubbish

Holly hurried along the pavement, the hood of her anorak pulled over her head. It was raining hard, but that wasn't why she was in a hurry.

Today her brother Tom was coming home!

He had been away four whole weeks, backpacking round India. With any luck he'd be there when she arrived.

And he had promised to bring her a present...

She started to run. Only one more street, turn the corner by the rubbish dump and – oops! She tripped over her shoelace.

Hastily she bent to tie it up. Hurry, hurry! Oh, she was useless at tying up laces. That's why they were always coming undone...

Mew! Mew!

What was that noise?

Holly stood up and listened.

Mew! Mew!

There it was again! It seemed to be coming from the rubbish dump. Should she go and look?

No, she was in too much of a hurry. She started to run, then stopped.

Perhaps she *should* go and look. It wouldn't take a minute. But the rubbish dump was all smelly and dirty. It wasn't a proper tip, just a piece of rough ground where people chucked things they didn't want. Bits of metal and old clothes and potato peelings. Disgusting stuff like that.

She listened again. The noise seemed to be coming from a cardboard box. She moved closer. Yes, the mewing was definitely coming from inside. She brushed off some potato peelings and lifted the lid. When she saw what was inside she gasped.

KITTENS!

She stared down at the three tiny creatures huddled together in the box. Someone must have thrown them away. Thrown them on the dump as if they were a bit of old rubbish. How could people be so *cruel*?

Two were black-and-white and one was grey-and-white. The little grey one tried to climb out of the box. Gently Holly pushed it back.

"Don't be frightened," she whispered. "You're safe now. I'll take care of you."

She closed the lid and carefully lifted the box. The kittens began to mew again. "I'm taking you home," she told them. "My brother Tom will be there and he's training to be a vet. He'll know what to do."

Mum met her at the door, beaming all over her face.

"Tom's here," she said. "He's had a wonderful time in India."

"Mum," Holly began, "you'll never guess what I just found…"

"Hello, Holly-pot." Tom came into the kitchen. He looked very tall and brown and fit. "What have you got in that box?"

"You'll never guess! I was passing the rubbish dump when I heard a noise, so I—"

"The rubbish dump?" Mum looked alarmed. "You picked that box up from the rubbish dump?"

"Yes, it was covered in potato peelings. And just look what's inside..." She opened the lid.

Mum and Tom peered into the box.

"Kittens!" exclaimed Mum.

"Pretty young, by the look of them," said Tom. "They can't be more than three or four weeks old."

"Someone must have thrown them away," said Holly. "How can people be so *cruel*?"

"I expect they were unwanted," said Mum.

"Well, they're not unwanted any more," said Holly. "We can keep them – can't we, Mum?"

"*Keep* them?" Mum sounded shocked. "Holly, we can't!"

"But you did say I could have a cat one day... "

"Yes, *one* cat – and *one* day. But not *three* cats – and not today." Mum sighed. "We'd better take them to the RSPCA. They'll know what to do with them."

"Oh, Mum!" Holly's eyes filled with tears. She couldn't bear to think of losing the kittens after she'd saved them from the rubbish dump.

"At that age they need special care," Tom said. "It's a job for experts."

"But you're training to be a vet," she reminded him. "You *are* an expert."

"Not yet." He shook his head. "Mum's right, Holly-pot. I'd better take them to the RSPCA."

"No!" Holly clutched the box to her chest.

Mum said, "Holly, Tom's been away a whole month and you haven't even said 'Welcome home'. Aren't you pleased to see him?"

"Yes, of course..."

"And he's brought you a lovely present. Show her, Tom."

Tom showed her a parcel wrapped in red and gold paper, but Holly didn't even glance at it. She went on clutching the cardboard box.

Mum said firmly, "Give those kittens to Tom and open your present."

"Yes, give them to me," said Tom. "I'll take them round straight away."

She didn't want to give him the kittens. She loved them, especially the little grey one. But she knew that he and Mum were right, they needed special care. It would be awful if they got sick because she couldn't look after them properly. So she gave Tom the box.

Then she snatched the parcel and ran upstairs to her room.

Later Tom came up to see her. "The kittens are safe now," he told her. "The RSPCA man said you could go and visit them if you like."

Holly sniffed. She hoped he wouldn't notice she'd been crying.

"Did you open your present?" he asked.

Holly nodded. She showed him the small wooden tiger she was holding in her hand. It had orange and black stripes and green eyes that glowed in the dark. "Thank you," she said. "It's lovely."

"But not as lovely as the kittens you found," Tom said. "I know how you feel, Holly-pot. But the kittens won't be ready to go to a new home for at least a month, so we've got plenty of time to make Mum change her mind."

Holly stared at him. "You mean … she might let me have them after all?"

"Not all three. But I'm pretty sure she'll let you have one of them."

"Oh, Tom!" She gave him a big, big hug. "I'm so glad you're home."

Chapter 2

Tyger, Tyger

Next day Tom took Holly to visit the kittens. "Do you mean the three that were left on the rubbish dump?" asked the RSPCA man.

"That's right," said Tom. "It was my sister who found them."

"I heard them mewing," said Holly. "They were in a box under some potato peelings. Some horrible person must have thrown them away."

He smiled at her. "Come with me."

He led them to a building marked "Cattery". Inside, a girl with fair hair tied back in a long pigtail was holding one of the kittens.

"Kathy looks after our orphans," the RSPCA man explained. "Kathy, this is the young lady who found the kittens that came in yesterday. She wants to know how they're getting on."

"They're getting on very well," she said. "At least, two of them are. But this one's very weak. I took him home last night to keep an eye on him."

Holly's heart sank. The kitten in Kathy's arms was the little grey one. "He's not going to die, is he?" she asked fearfully.

"I hope not," said Kathy. "But he won't touch solid food and he won't even feed from the bottle."

"He mustn't die," Holly said fiercely. "He's *my* kitten, so he's *got* to live."

Kathy looked at her in surprise. In fact Holly had surprised herself, but as soon as she saw him again she knew that he was the one she wanted.

"Holly's hoping to adopt one," Tom explained.

"In that case," said the RSPCA man, "we'd better put your name down for – what are you going to call him?"

"I don't know yet." She didn't want to give him a name until she was sure that he was going to live. And that Mum would let her have him.

"Plenty of time to decide," said the RSPCA man. "Now I must get back to the desk. Kathy can answer any

questions you have."

When he had gone Kathy said, "If he's going to be your kitten, Holly, perhaps you can make him feed from the bottle. Would you like to try?"

"Yes, please!"

He was so light, just a little bundle of fur and bones. Holly nursed him on her lap, stroking his ears.

Kathy gave her the feeding bottle.

"This is a special mixture," she explained. "It's a substitute for his mother's milk."

"Squeeze a little on to your finger," said Tom, "and hold it against his mouth."

She did as he said, but the kitten turned his head away.

"We reckon he's about four weeks old," said Kathy. "You found them just in time. They wouldn't have lasted much longer without food and warmth."

Tom began to stroke the other two kittens. "Why do you think they were dumped?" he asked Kathy.

She shrugged. "Who knows? So many careless people let their cats have kittens and then can't be bothered to look after them."

"In that case why don't they try to find homes for them?"

"Too much trouble, I suppose. Oh, look – he's feeding!"

Holly stared down at the kitten in her arms. At last he had begun to drink from the bottle. Even when she tried to move him into a more comfortable position he didn't stop.

Kathy laughed. "He's definitely your kitten, Holly! And it looks as if he's going to live after all."

Holly dared not move. She sat there, holding her breath while the kitten went on feeding.

On the way home she said to Tom, "Did you hear what Kathy said? He's definitely my kitten. But what if Mum goes on saying no?"

"Leave Mum to me," he said.

That afternoon her best friend Debra came over to play. They took the little wooden tiger Tom had brought her from India into the back garden and put it down in the long grass. If they lay on their fronts it was just like being in the jungle.

"Tom told me a sad thing about tigers," Holly said. "He says there are hardly any left in India. They've all been hunted and killed."

"I know a poem about a tiger," said Debra. "It goes:

Tyger, tyger, burning bright
In the forests of the night...

"That's all I can remember. The word 'tiger' is spelt funny, with a 'y' instead of an 'i'."

"Tyger, tyger..." Holly repeated, staring at the little wooden tiger stalking through the grass. It reminded her of the grey and white kitten, even though it was orange and black. They were both stripey ... and both cats.

A shadow fell over her. She looked up to see Tom.

"I thought you'd like to know," he said, "that Mum says yes."

Holly sat up with a start. "Yes to my kitten?"

"Yes to your kitten." He grinned at her. "Actually she didn't take much persuading. I think she'd already decided to let you have one of them."

Debra looked envious. "I wish I could have a kitten. My mum says I can but my dad thinks I wouldn't look after it properly."

"They do need a lot of looking after," Tom agreed. "Well, Holly-pot, now you'll have to think of a name for him."

But she already knew his name. "I shall call him Tyger," she said. "That's Tyger with a 'y'."

Chapter 3

Nine Lives

Holly went to visit Tyger about once a week. Soon he was eating proper kitten food and putting on weight fast.

"He's as greedy as his brother and sister," Kathy told her. "And every bit as rough when they're playing together."

Holly watched all three kittens chasing each other round the pen.

The other two had been given names as well. They were called Spud and Lucky – Spud because he'd been found under some potato peelings and Lucky because she was lucky to be alive.

"I wish I could adopt all three," she said with a sigh.

"Oh, I meant to tell you," said Kathy. "Spud and Lucky have found homes as well. Two families have already put their names down for them."

Holly was glad. Even though Tyger was special she cared just as much about the other two kittens. It was a relief to know they were going to be adopted too.

She picked Tyger up and gave him a cuddle. He looked up at her trustingly with his milky blue eyes. "I'm sure he knows me," she said. "I'm longing to take him home, but Tom says we've got to wait until he's at least eight weeks old."

42

"That's right," said Kathy. "And before then we have to arrange for someone to come and check your home."

Holly stared at her. "What do you mean – check my home?"

"We have to make sure it's a suitable place for a kitten to live. And that you'll be able to look after him properly." Kathy smiled. "Don't worry, I'm sure it will be all right."

But Holly couldn't help worrying.

What if they decided her home wasn't a suitable place for Tyger to live? Or that she wouldn't be able to look after him properly? She cuddled him closer and kissed the top of his furry head.

When she got home she told about it. But Mum only said, "They have to check up. After all, they don't know anything about us. I expect they want to make sure that Tyger will be in safe hands."

Holly's hands were safe, she knew that. But their house was small and so was the garden, especially at the front. And although the road where they lived was fairly quiet there were a lot of cars parked outside.

She asked Tom what he thought. He said, "Tyger will be as safe here as anywhere, Holly-pot. Anyway, aren't cats supposed to have nine lives?"

"Yes, but Tyger used up one of his when he was thrown on the rubbish dump," said Holly. "Nine minus one means he's only got eight left."

Tom laughed. "I reckon eight lives should be enough for anyone."

Luckily the woman who came from the RSPCA agreed with him. "I think Tyger will be very happy here," she said. "Now, have you thought of the things you will need before you collect him?"

Holly showed her the list she had made. It said:

1. A carrying box to fetch him home in.
2. A feeding bowl and some kitten food.
3. A litter tray and some litter.
4. A box lined with newspaper for him to sleep in.
5. A woolly jumper for him to curl up in.
6. Some toys for him to play with.

"That's excellent," said the RSPCA woman. "You'll need to keep him nice and quiet when he first arrives. Let him explore his new home – but don't forget to close all the doors and windows!"

Mum asked, "What about a cat flap? Should we have one put in the back door?"

"Not yet. You can do that later when he's older and more sensible." She stood up. "You'll be able to collect your kitten as soon as he's ready."

Holly couldn't believe it! Only another two weeks and Tyger would be hers. At last she could start getting everything ready to make him welcome. Oh, she just couldn't wait!

Chapter 4

Tyger Comes Home

As soon as Holly woke up that morning she knew something important was going to happen. But what was it...?

She sat up with a start.

TYGER WAS COMING HOME TODAY!

She had never washed and dressed

so quickly in her life. But then she had to wake Tom, who was terrible at getting up in the morning.

"Hurry up!" she urged, giving him a shake. "If we don't get there early someone else might take him."

Tom pulled the duvet over his head.

"Kathy wouldn't let that happen," he mumbled. "She knows he's your kitten."

"Yes, but – but something might go wrong!"

Tom groaned and threw off the duvet. "Oh, all right…"

They reached the RSPCA building with half an hour to spare. Kathy brought Tyger out and handed him over to Holly. "Here he is," she said. "Look after him well."

"I will," Holly promised. She placed the kitten carefully in the carrying box. "Soon be home," she whispered to him before closing the lid.

Kathy gave her an information sheet. "He'll need four meals a day at first," she said. "And two small drinks of milk mixed with water. We've already started him on a course of injections, but you'll need to register him with a vet fairly soon. The next one's due in three weeks' time."

"I'll arrange all that," said Tom.

"Good. And I've started his toilet training, but you'll have to be patient. It'll be a while yet before he uses the litter tray every time."

"I'll be very patient," Holly promised. To her surprise she saw that Kathy had tears in her eyes. "Are you sad because he's going away?"

Kathy nodded. "I always hate having to say goodbye to one of my orphans."

"You're welcome to come and visit him," said Tom.

Kathy smiled at him. "Thanks, I'd like to."

"What about Spud and Lucky?" Holly asked. "Are they going home today too?"

"Spud is," said Kathy. "But I'm afraid the people who were going to adopt Lucky have changed their minds. She'll have to stay here a while longer."

Holly was sad to hear this. On the way home she said to Tom, "Poor Lucky isn't so lucky after all. She'll be lonely without her brothers. You don't think Mum – ?"

"No, I don't," said Tom. "Anyway, you'll have your hands full with young Tyger here. He's going to need all your attention from now on."

When they got home she took the carrying box straight into the kitchen.

"Put it on the floor," said Tom, "and let him find his own way out."

"Wait!" said Mum. "Remember what the RSPCA woman said. Let's make sure that all the doors and windows are shut first."

Holly waited until Mum had shut the door into the hall. Then she gently opened the lid. Tyger was crouched on the blanket she had put inside the carrying box. He looked up at her, more curious than frightened.

Mum peered into the box. "He's grown! Last time I saw him he was a pathetic little scrap, but now he's a really healthy-looking kitten."

Holly felt proud. She watched Tyger trying to climb out of the box. He couldn't quite manage it by himself, so she had to help him. But once she had set him down on the floor he set off to explore on his short, wobbly legs.

"Look, Tyger, here's your bed…" She showed him the cardboard box lined with newspaper. "I've given you one of Mum's old jumpers to curl up in. And this is your litter tray…"

"*Very* important," said Tom.

"And this is your feeding bowl," Holly went on. "It's not very big but you can have a bigger one when you're older."

Tyger explored everywhere.
He explored under the
kitchen table, behind the
towel rail and over the
door mat. He climbed
on to Mum's feet and
climbed off again. He
climbed into his litter
tray and climbed out

again, leaving a trail of
litter behind him. Then
he explored all over
again, several times.

"You could try giving him a little
food," said Tom. "Not too much
because he's only got a
small stomach. Give
him some of that
baby cereal."

Tyger ate most of the
baby cereal. He took a
few sips of milk and

water from his drinking
bowl. He tried to wash
himself but nearly fell
over. Then he made a
puddle on the floor.

"Put him straight in the litter
tray," said Tom. "He'll soon
learn that's the
proper place for puddle-making."

Holly put him in the
litter tray. He climbed
straight out again and
into his bed.
Then he curled up
and went to sleep.

"Aah!" said Mum. "I expect he's tired. He's had a very busy day for a small kitten."

Holly sat on the floor beside Tyger's bed. She didn't want him to wake up and wonder where he was.

"Mum, you do like him, don't you?" she said. "You are glad he's come to live with us?"

"Very glad," said Mum. "In fact I think he was *meant* to come and live with us. That's why it was you who found him on the rubbish dump."

Holly nodded. But then she remembered there had been *three* kittens on the rubbish dump and one of them still hadn't found a home. Oh, if only someone would come along and adopt Lucky as well...

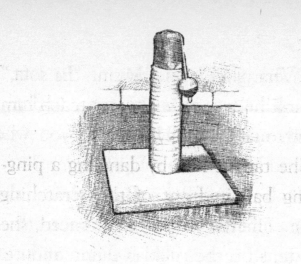

Chapter 5

Debra

Tyger loved to play. He played with ping-pong balls, screwed up paper, empty cotton reels, Mum's fingers and Holly's hair. But best of all he loved his scratching post.

Tom had made it out of a block of wood covered with a piece of old carpet. "With any luck this will stop

him sharpening his claws on the sofa,"
he said. "But you'll have to teach him
how to use it, Holly-pot."

She taught him by dangling a ping-
pong ball in front of the scratching
post. Then, when Tyger pounced, she
snatched it away at the last minute.
He soon found out how good it felt
when his claws sank into the soft
carpet. Before long he was
stretching further and
further up the
post, digging his
claws in and out
with a blissful
look on his
face.

Holly's best friend Debra came round nearly every day to see him. She loved helping to feed him and even took turns in cleaning out his litter tray. Most of all she loved to nurse him and stroke his silky fur.

"He's so beautiful," she said. "You are lucky, Holly."

"Yes, I know," Holly said. "But he can be quite naughty sometimes. This morning he climbed up the curtain and couldn't get down again. He just swung there, mewing like mad, and I had to come and rescue him."

"He could be as naughty as he liked if he was mine," said Debra with a sigh. "I wouldn't get cross with him, ever."

"I don't get cross with him," said Holly. "But I have to teach him how to behave. You see, he was very young when he lost his mother, so he has to learn from human beings. First it was Kathy at the RSPCA, and now it's me."

"What about hunting?" asked Debra. "Will you teach him to catch mice and things?"

"No, I won't!" said Holly. "But if he does catch something and brings it home I shan't tell him off either. Tom says you can't stop cats hunting. It's their natural instinct."

Debra stroked Tyger's ears. "Can we take him into the garden?"

"Not yet. We've got to wait until he's had all his flu injections."

"Poor Tyger," said Debra. "I've had a flu injection and it *hurt!*"

"Cat flu can be really serious," said Holly. "Cats can die of it if they haven't been vaccinated."

Debra looked horrified. She hugged Tyger close as if she wanted to protect him. But Tyger didn't much like being hugged. He wriggled free and jumped to the ground.

At that moment the doorbell rang. Holly picked Tyger up before he could dash into the hall. "I wonder who that is?" she said.

Tom put his head round the door. "It's Kathy from the RSPCA," he said. "She's come to visit Tyger."

Debra went pale. "Do you think she's come to take him back?" she asked Holly in a loud whisper.

"Don't worry." Laughing, Kathy came into the room. "I just wanted to see how he's getting along, that's all."

"He's getting along fine. Look…"
Holly put Tyger into Kathy's arms.

"Wow!" she exclaimed. "Can this be the same kitten who arrived at the Centre in a cardboard box? Who was a real little scaredy-cat when he was a baby? Now he's bold as brass – and twice as heavy!"

Tyger dabbed Kathy's chin with his paw. She laughed again. "They say cats always fall on their feet and Tyger certainly has. I reckon he's a very lucky little cat."

The word "lucky" made Holly think of Tyger's sister. "Has Lucky found a home yet?" she asked.

Kathy shook her head. "I'm afraid we've got rather a lot of kittens in the cattery at the moment, which means that people have plenty to choose from. So far nobody seems to want Lucky."

Debra went pink. "I do," she said. "I want Lucky."

Holly stared at her. "But you've never even *seen* Lucky. How do you know you want her?"

"Because I do." Debra went even pinker. "I want her really badly."

"Perhaps you should come and look at her first," Kathy said gently. "She's not exactly like Tyger, you know. She's black and white..."

"Hang on a minute," said Tom. "Hasn't Debra already asked her parents if she could have a kitten? And didn't her dad say no?"

"Yes, but her mum said she could have one." Holly began to feel excited. It would be wonderful if Debra could give Lucky a home!

"And my dad only said no because he thought I wouldn't know how to look after it," Debra explained. "But I do now. I've watched how Holly looks after Tyger. I know exactly what to do."

"In that case," said Tom, "perhaps you'd better ask him again."

Debra nodded. "I'll ask him as soon as he gets home this evening."

Holly could hardly wait!

But by the time evening came she had forgotten all about Debra having Lucky. Because something terrible had happened.

Tyger had gone missing...

MISSING
'Tyger'

Chapter 6

Missing!

"He can't have gone far," said Tom when she told him. "Where did you last see him, Holly-pot?"

"In the kitchen." Holly blinked back her tears. "He was under the table while I was having my tea."

"Did anyone leave the back door open?"

"No, I'm sure we didn't." Mum looked as upset as Holly. "We wouldn't be so careless."

"In that case he must still be in the house."

"But I've searched every room," said Holly. "And he usually comes when I call his name."

"Perhaps he's shut in somewhere. Have you looked in the cupboard under the stairs?"

Holly nodded. "He wasn't there."

"Look again," said Tom.

They were in the middle of looking again when Debra knocked on the front door.

"You'll never guess!" she said excitedly when Holly let her in. "This afternoon Mum and I went to the RSPCA to see Lucky. And Mum loved her just as much as I did, so we put our name down for her. And when Dad came home Mum told him all about Lucky and how much we both wanted her and guess what! Dad said yes."

Holly tried to look pleased. "I'm glad..."

"We're going to fetch her next Saturday. I bet Tyger will be pleased to see his sister again. They'll be able to play together..." Suddenly Debra noticed Holly's tearful face. "What's the matter?"

"Tyger's gone missing," said Holly.

Debra looked horrified. "Do you mean he's run away?"

"I don't know," Holly said helplessly. "We've looked everywhere but there's no sign of him."

"My mum always says that if you lose something you nearly always find it in the most obvious place," said Debra. "Where did you last see him?"

"In the kitchen." Holly sniffed. "Under the table."

"Come on. Let's look again."

They went into the kitchen and looked under the table. No Tyger.

Then Debra gave a little shriek. She pointed at the glass front of the washing-machine. "What's that?"

It was a face. A small striped face peering anxiously out of the window...

"*Tyger!*" Holly opened the loading door. She picked him up in her arms. "Mum! Tom! We've found him!"

They both came rushing into the kitchen. "Where was he?" asked Tom.

"In the washing-machine. He must have climbed in and gone to sleep. And then someone shut the door..."

"I did," said Mum. "I noticed it was open as I walked past. A little while earlier I'd thrown a dirty towel in there, ready to wash. Tyger must have curled up on it..." She sank on to a chair, looking pale. "Oh, thank goodness I didn't switch it on!"

"You wouldn't have switched it on for just one towel," Tom pointed out. "We'd have found him – eventually. Still, it shows how you have to be extra, extra careful when there's a kitten around, especially about shutting doors."

Holly hugged Tyger. "It was Debra who found him," she said. "She came to tell us her dad's changed his mind. He says she can have Lucky after all!"

"That's great news, Debra," said Tom. "Well, now the excitement's over I must get ready to go out. I'm meeting Kathy at seven."

"Kathy from the RSPCA?" asked Holly.

"That's right. We're going to see a film about endangered animals." He grinned and tickled Tyger under the chin. "It's a good thing this one started out with nine lives. At this rate he's going to need all of them."

"Could you please tell Kathy my dad's said yes?" said Debra.

"I'll tell her," Tom promised.

Holly hugged Tyger even tighter.

She couldn't help thinking that if she hadn't stopped beside the rubbish dump that day ... and if she hadn't heard the mewing ... and if she hadn't looked inside the cardboard box ... how different life would be for all of them, especially the kittens.

What a good thing she was useless at tying up shoe-laces!

The End